Celebration

by Harold Pinter

MUSIC USE NOTE

IMPORTANT BILLING AND CREDIT REQUIREMENTS

(NAME OF PRODUCER)

presents

CELEBRATION

by Harold Pinter

CELEBRATION
by
Harold Pinter

was first presented by the Almeida Theatre Company at the

Almeida Theatre, London,
on 16 March 2000.

<u>Cast:</u>

Lambert	Keith Allen
Julie	Susan Wooldridge
Matt	Andy de la Tour
Prue	Lindsay Duncan
Russell	Steven Pacey
Suki	Lia Williams
Richard	Thomas Wheatley
Waiter	Danny Dyer
Sonia	Indira Varma
Waitress 1	Nina Raine
Waitress 2	Katherine Tozer

Directed by Harold Pinter
Designer: Eileen Diss
Lighting: Mark Hughes
Costume: Dany Everett
Sound: John Leonard

CHARACTERS

LAMBERT

JULIE

MATT

PRUE

} all in their forties

RUSSELL, a man in his thirties

SUKI, a woman of twenty-eight

RICHARD, a man in his fifties

WAITER, a man of twenty-five

SONIA, a woman in her thirties

(Scene: A restaurant. Two curved banquettes. LAMBERT, JULIE, MATT, and PRUE sit at one banquette, RUSSELL and SUKI at the other.)

TABLE ONE

WAITER. Who's having the duck?
LAMBERT. The duck's for me.
JULIE. No it isn't.
LAMBERT. No it isn't. Who's it for?
JULIE. Me.
LAMBERT. What am I having? I thought I was having the duck.
JULIE. *(To WAITER.)* The duck's for me.
MATT. *(To WAITER.)* Chicken for my wife, steak for me.
WAITER. Chicken for the lady.
PRUE. Thank you so much.
WAITER. And who's having the steak?
MATT. Me. *(He picks up a wine bottle and pours.)* Here we are. Frascati for the ladies. And Valpolicella for me.
LAMBERT. And for me. I mean, what about me? What did I order? I haven't the faintest idea. What did I order?
JULIE. Who cares?
LAMBERT. Who cares? I bloody care.
PRUE. Osso buco.
LAMBERT. Osso what?
PRUE. Buco.
MATT. It's an old Italian dish.
LAMBERT. I knew *osso* was Italian but I know bugger-all about *bucco.*
MATT. I didn't know arsehole was Italian.
LAMBERT. Yes, but on the other hand what's the Italian for

arsehole?
>PRUE. Julie, Lambert. Happy anniversary.
>MATT. Cheers.

(They lift their glasses and drink.)

TABLE TWO

RUSSELL. They believe in me.

SUKI. Who do?

RUSSELL. They do. What do you mean, who do? They do.

SUKI. Oh, do they?

RUSSELL. Yes, they believe in me. They reckon me. They're investing in me. In my *nous*. They believe in me.

SUKI. Listen. I believe in you. Honestly. I do. No really, honestly. I'm sure they believe in you. And they're right to believe in you. I mean, listen, I want you to be rich, believe me. I want you to be rich so that you can buy me houses and panties and I'll know that you really love me.

(They drink.)

RUSSELL. Listen, she was just a secretary. That's all. No more.

SUKI. Like me.

RUSSELL. What do you mean like you? She was nothing like you.

SUKI. I was a secretary once.

RUSSELL. She was a scrubber. A scrubber. They're all the same, these secretaries, these scrubbers. They're like politicians. They love power, they use it. They go home, they get on the phone, they tell their girlfriends, they have a good laugh. Listen to me. I'm being honest. You won't find many like me. I fell for it. I've admitted it. She just twisted me round her little finger.

SUKI. That's funny. I thought she twisted you round *your* little finger.

(Pause.)

RUSSELL. You don't know what these girls are like. Those secretaries.

SUKI. Oh I think I do.

RUSSELL. You don't.

SUKI. Oh I do.

RUSSELL. What do you mean, you do?

SUKI. I've been behind a few filing cabinets.

RUSSELL. What?

SUKI. In my time. When I was a plump young secretary. I know what the back of a filing cabinet looks like.

RUSSELL. Oh, do you?

SUKI. Oh yes. Listen, I would invest in you myself if I had any money. Do you know why? Because I believe in you.

RUSSELL. What's all this about filing cabinets?

SUKI. Oh, that was when I was a plump young secretary. I would never do all those things now. Never. Out of the question. You see, the trouble was I was so excitable, their excitement made me so excited, but I would never do all those things now I'm a grown-up woman and not a silly young thing, a silly and dizzy young girl, such a naughty, saucy, flirty, giggly young thing; sometimes I could hardly walk from one filing cabinet to another I was so excited, I was so plump and wobbly it was terrible, men simply couldn't keep their hands off me, their demands were outrageous but coming back to more important things, they're right to believe in you; why shouldn't they believe in you?

TABLE ONE

JULIE. I've always told him. Always. But he doesn't listen. I tell him all the time. But he doesn't listen.

PRUE. You mean he just doesn't listen?

JULIE. I tell him all the time.

PRUE. *(To LAMBERT.)* Why don't you listen to your wife? She stands by you through thick and thin. You've got a loyal wife there and never forget it.

LAMBERT. I've got a loyal wife where?

PRUE. Here! At this table.

LAMBERT. I've got one under the table, take my tip. *(He looks under the table.)* Christ. She's really loyal under the table. Always has been. You wouldn't believe it.

JULIE. Why don't you go and buy a new car and drive it into a brick wall?

LAMBERT. She loves me.

MATT. No, she loves new cars.

LAMBERT. With soft leather seats.

MATT. There was a song once.

LAMBERT. How did it go?

MATT.

"Ain't she neat?
Ain't she neat?
As she's walking up the street.
She's got a lovely bubbly pair of tits
And a soft leather seat."

LAMBERT. That's a really beautiful song.

MATT. I've always admired that song. You know what it is? It's a traditional folk song.

LAMBERT. It's got class.

MATT. It's got tradition and class.

LAMBERT. They don't grow on trees.

MATT. Too bloody right.

LAMBERT. Hey, Matt!

MATT. What?

(LAMBERT picks up the bottle of Valpolicella. It is empty.)

LAMBERT. There's something wrong with this bottle.

(MATT turns and calls.)

MATT. Waiter!

TABLE TWO

RUSSELL. All right. Tell me. Do you think I have a nice character?

SUKI. Yes, I think you do. I think you do. I mean I think you do. Well ... I mean ... I think you could have quite a nice character but the trouble is that when you come down to it you haven't actually got any character to begin with — I mean as such, that's the thing.

RUSSELL. As such?

SUKI. Yes, the thing is you haven't really got any character at all, have you? As such. *Au fond.* But I wouldn't worry about it. For example, look at me. I don't have any character either. I'm just a reed. I'm just a reed in the wind. Aren't I? You know I am. I'm just a reed in the wind.

RUSSELL. You're a whore.

SUKI. A whore in the wind.

RUSSELL. With the wind blowing up your skirt.

SUKI. That's right. How did you know? How did you know the sensation? I didn't know that men could possibly know about that kind of thing. I mean men don't wear skirts. So I didn't think men could possibly know what it was like when the wind blows up a girl's skirt. Because men don't wear skirts.

RUSSELL. You're a prick.

SUKI. Not quite.

RUSSELL. You're a prick.

SUKI. good gracious. Am I really?

RUSSELL. Yes. That's what you are really.

SUKI. Am I really?

RUSSELL. Yes. That's what you are really.

TABLE ONE

LAMBERT. What's the other song you know? The one you said was a classic.

MATT.

"Wash me in the water
 Where you washed your dirty daughter."

LAMBERT. That's it. *(To JULIE:)* Know that one?

JULIE. It's not in my repertoire, darling.

LAMBERT. This is the best restaurant in town. That's what they say.

MATT. That's what they say.

LAMBERT. This is a piss-up dinner. Do you know how much money I made last year?

MATT. I know this is a piss-up dinner.

LAMBERT. It is a piss-up dinner.

PRUE. *(To JULIE.)* His mother always hated me. The first time she saw me she hated me. She never gave me one present in the whole of her life. Nothing. She wouldn't give me the drippings off her nose.

JULIE. I know.

PRUE. The drippings off her nose. Honestly.

JULIE. All mothers-in-law are like that. They love their sons. They love their boys. They don't want their sons to be fucked by other girls. Isn't that right?

PRUE. Absolutely. All mothers want their sons to be fucked by themselves.

JULIE. By their mothers.

PRUE. All mothers —

LAMBERT. All mothers want to be fucked by their mothers.

MATT. Or by themselves.

PRUE. No, you've got it the wrong way round.

LAMBERT. How's that?

MATT. All mothers want to be fucked by their sons.

LAMBERT. Now wait a minute —

MATT. My point is —

LAMBERT. No, my point is — how old do you have to be?

JULIE. To be what?
LAMBERT. To be fucked by your mother.
MATT. Any age, mate. Any age.

(They all drink.)

LAMBERT. How did you enjoy your dinner, darling?
JULIE. I wasn't impressed.
LAMBERT. You weren't impressed?
JULIE. No.
LAMBERT. I bring her to the best caff in town — spending a fortune — and she's not impressed.
MATT. Don't forget this is your anniversary. That's why we're here.
LAMBERT. What anniversary?
PRUE. It's your wedding anniversary.
LAMBERT. All I know is this is the most expensive fucking restaurant in town and she's not impressed.

(RICHARD comes to the table.)

RICHARD. Good evening.
MATT. Good evening.
PRUE. Good evening.
JULIE. Good evening.
LAMBERT. Good evening, Richard. How you been?
RICHARD. Very very well. Been to a play?
MATT. No. The ballet.
RICHARD. Oh, the ballet. What was it?
LAMBERT. That's a fucking good question.
MATT. It's unanswerable.
RICHARD. Good, was it?
LAMBERT. Unbelievable.
JULIE. What ballet?
MATT. None of them could reach the top notes. Could they?
RICHARD. Good dinner?
MATT. Fantastic.

LAMBERT. Top-notch. Gold-plated.
PRUE. Delicious.
LAMBERT. My wife wasn't impressed.
RICHARD. Oh, really?
JULIE. I liked the waiter.
RICHARD. Which one?
JULIE. The one with the fur-lined jockstrap.
LAMBERT. He takes it off for breakfast.
JULIE. Which is more than you do.
RICHARD. Well, how nice to see you all.
PRUE. She wasn't impressed with her food. It's true. She said so. She thought it was dry as dust. She said — what did you say, darling? — she's my sister — she said she could cook better than that with one hand stuffed between her legs; she said — no, honestly — she said she could make a better sauce than the one on that plate if she pissed into it. Don't think she was joking — she's my sister, I've known her all my life, all my life, since we were little innocent girls, all our lives, when we were babies, when we used to lie in the nursery and hear Mummy beating the shit out of Daddy. We saw the blood on the sheets the next day — when Nanny was in the pantry — my sister and me — and Nanny was in the pantry — and the pantry maid was in the larder and the parlor maid was in the laundry room washing the blood out of the sheets. That's how my little sister and I were brought up and she could make a better sauce than yours if she pissed into it.
MATT. Well, it's lovely to be here, I'll say that.
LAMBERT. Lovely to be here.
JULIE. Lovely, lovely.
MATT. Really lovely.
RICHARD. Thank you.

(PRUE stands and goes to RICHARD.)

PRUE. Can I thank you? Can I thank you personally? I'd like to thank you myself, in my own way.
RICHARD. Well, thank you.
PRUE. No, no, I'd really like to thank you in a very personal way.
JULIE. She'd like to give you her personal thanks.

PRUE. Will you let me kiss you? I'd like to kiss you on the mouth.

JULIE. That's funny. I'd like to kiss him on the mouth too. *(She stands and goes to him.)* Because I've been maligned, I've been misrepresented. I never said I didn't like your sauce. I love your sauce.

PRUE. We can't both kiss him on the mouth at the same time.

LAMBERT. You could tickle his arse with a feather.

RICHARD. Well, I'm so glad. I'm really glad. See you later I hope.

(RICHARD goes. PRUE and JULIE sit. Silence.)

MATT. Charming man.

LAMBERT. That's why this is the best and most expensive restaurant in the whole of Europe — because he *insists* upon proper standards, he *insists* that standards are maintained up to the highest standards, up to the very highest fucking standards —

MATT. He doesn't jib.

LAMBERT. Jib? Of course he doesn't jib — it would be more than his life was worth. He jibs at nothing!

PRUE. I knew him in the old days.

MATT. What do you mean?

PRUE. When he was a chef.

(LAMBERT's mobile phone rings.)

LAMBERT. Who the fuck's this? *(He switches it on.)* Yes? What? *(He listens briefly.)* I said no calls! It's my fucking wedding anniversary! *(He switches it off.)* Cunt.

TABLE TWO

SUKI. I'm so proud of you.

RUSSELL. Yes?

SUKI. And I know these people are good people. These people who believe in you. They're good people. Aren't they?

RUSSELL. Very good people.

SUKI. And when I meet them, when you introduce me to them, they'll treat me with respect, won't they? They won't want to fuck me behind a filing cabinet?

(SONIA comes to the table.)

SONIA. Good evening.

RUSSELL. Good evening.

SUKI. Good evening.

SONIA. Everything all right?

RUSSELL. Wonderful.

SONIA. No complaints?

RUSSELL. Absolutely no complaints whatsoever. Absolutely numero uno all along the line.

SONIA. What a lovely compliment.

RUSSELL. Heartfelt.

SONIA. Been to the theatre?

SUKI. The opera.

SONIA. Oh, really, what was it?

SUKI. Well ... there was a lot going on. A lot of singing. A great deal, as a matter of fact. They never stopped. Did they?

RUSSELL. *(To SONIA.)* Listen, let me ask you something.

SONIA. You can ask me absolutely anything you like.

RUSSELL. What was your upbringing?

SONIA. That's funny. Everybody asks me that. Everybody seems to find that an interesting subject. I don't know why. Isn't it funny? So many people express curiosity about my upbringing. I've no idea why. What you really mean of course is how did I arrive in the position I hold now — *maîtresse d'hôtel* — isn't that right? Isn't that your question? Well, I was born in Bethnal Green. My mother was a chiropo-dist. I had no father.

RUSSELL. Fantastic.

SONIA. Are you going to try our bread-and-butter pudding?

RUSSELL. In spades. *(SONIA smiles and goes.)* Did I ever tell you about my mother's bread-and-butter pudding?

SUKI You never have. Please tell me.

RUSSELL. You really want me to tell you? You're not being in-sincere?

SUKI. Darling. Give me your hand. There. I have your hand. I'm holding your hand. Now please tell me. Please tell me about your mother's bread-and-butter pudding. What was it like?

RUSSELL. It was like drowning in an ocean of richness.

SUKI. How beautiful. You're a poet.

RUSSELL. I wanted to be a poet once. But I got no encourage-ment from my dad. He thought I was an arsehole.

SUKI. He was jealous of you, that's all. He saw you as a threat. He thought you wanted to steal his wife.

RUSSELL. His wife?

SUKI. Well, you know what they say.

RUSSELL. What?

SUKI. Oh, you know what they say.

(The WAITER comes to the table and pours wine.)

WAITER. Do you mind if I interject?

RUSSELL. Eh?

WAITER. I say, do you mind if I make an interjection?

SUKI. We'd welcome it.

WAITER. It's just that I heard you talking about T. S. Eliot a lit-tle bit earlier this evening.

SUKI. Oh, you heard that, did you?

WAITER. I did. And I thought you might be interested to know that my grandfather knew T. S. Eliot quite well.

SUKI. Really?

WAITER. I'm not claiming that he was a close friend of his, but he was a damn sight more that a nodding acquaintance. He knew them

all, in fact, Ezra Pound, W. H. Auden, C. Day-Lewis, Louis Mac-
Neice, Stephen Spender, George Barker, Dylan Thomas, and if you go
back a few years he was a bit of a drinking companion of D. H. Law-
rence, Joseph Conrad, Ford Madox Ford, W. B. Yeats, Aldous Hux-
ley, Virginia Woolf, and Thomas Hardy in his dotage. My grandfather
was carving out a niche for himself in politics at the time. Some saw
him as a future Chancellor of the Exchequer or at least First Lord of
the Admiralty but he decided instead to command a battalion in the
Spanish Civil War but as things turned out he spent most of his spare
time in the United States where he was a very close pal of Ernest
Hemingway — they used to play gin rummy together until the cows
came home. But he was also boon compatriots with William Faulkner,
Scott Fitzgerald, Upton Sinclair, John Dos Passos — you know, that
whole vivid Chicago gang — not to mention John Steinbeck, Erskine
Caldwell, Carson McCullers, and other members of the old Deep
South conglomerate. I mean — what I'm trying to say is — that as a
man my grandfather was just about as all-round as you can get. He
was never without his pocket Bible and he was a dab hand at pocket
billiards. He stood four-square in the center of the intellectual and lit-
erary life of the tens, twenties, and thirties. He was James Joyce's
godmother.

(Silence.)

RUSSELL. Have you been working here long?
WAITER. Years.
RUSSELL. You going to stay until it changes hands?
WAITER. Are you suggesting that I'm about to get the boot?
SUKI. They wouldn't do that to a nice lad like you.
WAITER. To be brutally honest, I don't think I'd recover if they
did a thing like that. This place is like a womb to me. I prefer to stay
in my womb. I strongly prefer that to being born.
RUSSELL. I don't blame you. Listen, next time we're talking
about T. S. Eliot I'll drop you a card.
WAITER. You would make me a very happy man. Thank you.
Thank you. You are incredibly gracious people.
SUKI. How sweet of you.

WAITER. Gracious and graceful.

(He goes.)

SUKI. What a nice young man.

TABLE ONE

LAMBERT. You won't believe this. You're not going to believe this — I'm only saying this because I'm among friends — and I know I'm well liked because I trust my family and my friends — because I know they like me fundamentally — you know, deep down they trust me, deep down they respect me — otherwise I wouldn't say this. I wouldn't take you all into my confidence if I thought you all hated my guts — I couldn't be open and honest with you if I thought you thought I was a pile of shit. If I thought you would like to see me hung, drawn and fucking quartered — I could never be frank and honest with you if that was the truth — never .... *(Silence.)* But as I was about to say, you won't believe this. I fell in love once and this girl I fell in love with loved me back. I know she did.

(Pause.)

JULIE. Wasn't that me, darling?
LAMBERT. Who?
MATT. Her.
LAMBERT. Her? No, not her. A girl. I used to take her for walks along the river.
JULIE. Lambert fell in love with me on the top of a bus. It was a short journey. Fulham Broadway to Shepherd's Bush, but it was enough. He was trembling all over. I remember. *(To PRUE.)* When I got home I came and sat on your bed, didn't I?
LAMBERT. I used to take this girl for walks along the river. I was young. I wasn't much more than a nipper.
MATT. That's funny. I never knew anything about that. And I knew you quite well, didn't I?
LAMBERT. What do you mean you knew me quite well? You knew nothing about me. You know nothing about me. Who the fuck are you anyway?
MATT. I'm your big brother.
LAMBERT. I'm talking about love, mate. You know, real fucking love, walking along the banks of a river holding hands.

MATT. I saw him the day he was born. You know what he looked like? An alcoholic. Pissed as a newt. He could hardly stand.

JULIE. He was trembling like a leaf on top of that bus. I'll never forget it.

PRUE. I was there when you came home. I remember what you said. You came into my room. You sat down on my bed.

MATT. What did she say?

PRUE. I mean we were sisters, weren't we?

MATT. Well, what did she say?

PRUE. I'll never forget what you said. You sat on my bed. Didn't you? Do you remember?

LAMBERT. This girl was in love with me — I'm trying to tell you.

PRUE. Do you remember what you said?

TABLE TWO

(RICHARD comes to the table.)

RICHARD. Good evening.
RUSSELL. Good evening.
SUKI. Good evening.
RICHARD. Everything in order?
RUSSELL. First class.
RICHARD. I'm so glad.
SUKI. Can I say something?
RICHARD. But indeed —
SUKI. Everyone is so happy in your restaurant. I mean women and men. You make people so happy.
RICHARD. Well, we do like to feel that it's a happy restaurant.
RUSSELL. It is a happy restaurant. For example, look at me. Look at me. I'm basically a totally disordered personality; some people would describe me as a psychopath. *(To SUKI.)* Am I right?
SUKI. Yes.
RUSSELL. But when I'm sitting in the restaurant I suddenly find I have no psychopathic tendencies at all. I don't feel like killing everyone in sight. I don't feel like putting a bomb under everyone's arse. I feel something quite different. I have a sense of equilibrium, of harmony, I love my fellow diners. Now this is very unusual for me. Normally I feel — as I've just said — absolute malice and hatred towards everyone within spitting distance — but here I feel love. How do you explain it?
SUKI. It's the ambience.
RICHARD. Yes. I think ambience is that intangible thing that cannot be defined.
RUSSELL. Quite right.
SUKI. It is intangible. You're absolutely right.
RUSSELL. Absolutely.
RICHARD. That is absolutely right. But it does — I would freely admit — exist. It's something you find you are part of. Without knowing exactly what it is.

RUSSELL. Yes. I had an old schoolmaster once who used to say that ambience surrounds you. He never stopped saying that. He lived in a little house in a nice little village but none of us boys were ever invited to tea.

RICHARD. Yes, it's funny you should say that. I was brought up in a little village myself.

SUKI. No? Were you?

RICHARD. Yes, isn't it odd? In a little village in the country.

RUSSELL. What, right in the country?

RICHARD. Oh, absolutely. And my father once took me to our village pub. I was only that high. Too young to join him for his pint, of course. But I did look in. Black beams.

RUSSELL. On the roof?

RICHARD. Well, holding the ceiling up in fact. Old men smoking pipes, no music of course, cheese rolls, gherkins, happiness. I think this restaurant — which you so kindly patronize — was inspired by that pub in my childhood. I do hope you noticed that you have complimentary gherkins as soon as you take your seat.

SUKI. That was you! That was your idea!

RICHARD. I believe the concept of this restaurant rests in that public house of my childhood.

SUKI. I find that incredibly moving.

TABLE ONE

LAMBERT. I'd like to raise my glass.

MATT. What to?

LAMBERT. To my wife. To our anniversary.

JULIE. Oh, darling! You remembered!

LAMBERT. I'd like to raise my glass. I ask you to raise your glasses to my wife.

JULIE. I'm so touched by this, honestly. I mean, I have to say —

LAMBERT. Raise your fucking glass and shut up!

JULIE. But darling, that's naked aggression. He doesn't normally go in for naked aggression. He usually disguises it under honeyed words. What is it, sweetie? He's got a cold in the nose, that's what it is.

LAMBERT. I want us to drink to our anniversary. We've been married for more bloody years than I can remember and it don't seem a day too long.

PRUE. Cheers.

MATT. Cheers.

JULIE. It's funny our children aren't here. When they were young we spent so much time with them, the little things, looking after them.

PRUE. I know.

JULIE. Playing with them.

PRUE. Feeding them.

JULIE. Being their mothers.

PRUE. They always loved me much more than they loved him.

JULIE. Me too. They loved me to distraction. I was their mother.

PRUE. Yes, I was too. I was my children's mother.

MATT. They have no memory.

LAMBERT. Who?

MATT. Children. They have no memory. They remember nothing. They don't remember who their father was or who their mother was. It's all a hole in the wall for them. They don't remember their own life.

(SONIA comes to the table.)

SONIA. Everything all right?

JULIE. Perfect.

SONIA. Were you at the opera this evening?

JULIE. No.

PRUE. No.

SONIA. Theatre?

PRUE. No.

JULIE. No.

MATT. This is a celebration.

SONIA. Oh my goodness! A birthday?

MATT. Anniversary.

PRUE. My sister and her husband. Anniversary of their marriage. I was her leading bridesmaid.

MATT. I was his best man.

LAMBERT. I was just about to fuck her at the altar when somebody stopped me.

SONIA. Really?

MATT. I stopped him. His zip went down and I kicked him up the arse. It would have been a scandal. The world's press was on the doorstep.

JULIE. He was always impetuous.

SONIA. We get so many different kinds of people in here, people from all walks of life.

PRUE. Do you really?

SONIA. Oh yes. People from all walks of life. People from different countries. I've often said, "You don't have to speak English to enjoy good food." I've often said that. Or even understand English. It's like sex, isn't it? You don't have to be English to enjoy sex. You don't have to speak English to enjoy sex. Lots of people enjoy sex without being English. I've known one or two Belgian people, for example, who love sex and they don't speak a word of English. The same applies to Hungarians.

LAMBERT. Yes. I met a chap who was born in Venezuela once and he didn't speak a fucking word of English.

MATT. Did he enjoy sex?

LAMBERT. Sex?

SONIA. Yes, it's funny you should say that. I met a man from

Morocco once and he was very interested in sex.

JULIE. What happened to him?

SONIA. Now you've upset me. I think I'm going to cry.

PRUE. Oh, poor dear. Did he let you down?

SONIA. He's dead. He died in another woman's arms. He was on the job. Can you see how tragic my life has been?

(Pause.)

MATT. Well, I can. I don't know about the others.

JULIE. I can too.

PRUE. So can I.

SONIA. Have a happy night.

(She goes.)

LAMBERT. Lovely woman.

(The waiter comes to the table and pours wine into their glasses.)

WAITER. Do you mind if I interject?

MATT. What?

WAITER. Do you mind if I make an interjection.

MATT. Help yourself.

WAITER. It's just that a little bit earlier I heard you saying something about the Hollywood studio system in the thirties.

PRUE. Oh, you heard that?

WAITER. Yes. And I thought you might be interested to know that my grandfather was very familiar with a lot of the old Hollywood film stars back in those days. He used to knock about with Clark Gable and Elisha Cook, Jr. and he was one of the very few native-born Englishmen to have had it off with Hedy Lamarr.

JULIE. No!

LAMBERT. What was she like in the sack?

WAITER. He said she was really tasty.

JULIE. I'll bet she was.

WAITER. Of course there was a very well established Irish Mafia in Hollywood in those days. And there was a very close connection between some of the famous Irish film stars and some of the famous Irish gangsters in Chicago. Al Capone and Victor Mature, for example. The were both Irish. Then there was John Dillinger, the celebrated gangster, and Gary Cooper, the celebrated film star. They were Jewish.

(Silence.)

JULIE. It makes you think, doesn't it?
PRUE. It does make you think.
LAMBERT. You see the girl at that table? I know her. I fucked her when she was eighteen.
JULIE. What, by the banks of the river?

(LAMBERT waves at SUKI. SUKI waves back. SUKI whispers to RUSSELL, gets up, and goes to LAMBERT's table, followed by RUSSELL.)

SUKI. Lambert! It's you!
LAMBERT. Suki! You remember me!
SUKI. Do you remember me?
LAMBERT. Do I remember you? *Do* I remember you!
SUKI. This is my husband, Russell.
LAMBERT. Hello, Russell.
RUSSELL. Hello, Lambert.
LAMBERT. This is my wife, Julie.
JULIE. Hello, Suki.
SUKI. Hello, Julie.
RUSSELL. Hello, Julie.
JULIE. Hello, Russell.
LAMBERT. And this is my brother, Matt.
MATT. Hello, Suki, hello, Russell.
SUKI. Hello, Matt.
RUSSELL. Hello, Matt.
LAMBERT. And this is his wife, Prue. She's Julie's sister.
SUKI. She's not!

PRUE. Yes, we're sisters and they're brothers.
SUKI. They're not!
RUSSELL. Hello, Prue.
PRUE. Hello, Russell.
SUKI. Hello, Prue.
PRUE. Hello, Suki.
LAMBERT. Sit down. Squeeze in. Have a drink. *(They sit.)* What'll you have?
RUSSELL. A drop of that red wine would work wonders.
LAMBERT. Suki?
RUSSELL. She'll have the same.
SUKI. *(To LAMBERT.)* Are you still obsessed with gardening?
LAMBERT. Me?
SUKI. *(To JULIE.)* When I knew him he was absolutely obsessed with gardening.
LAMBERT. Yes, well, I would say I'm still moderately obsessed with gardening.
JULIE. He likes grass.
LAMBERT. It's true. I love grass.
JULIE. Green grass.
SUKI. You used to love flowers, didn't you? Do you still love flowers?
JULIE. He adores flowers. The other day I saw him emptying a piss pot into a bowl of lilies.
RUSSELL. My dad was a gardener.
MATT. Not your grandad?
Russell. No, my dad.
SUKI. That's right, he was. He was always walking about with a lawn mower.
LAMBERT. What, even in the Old Kent Road?
RUSSELL. He was a man of the soil.
MATT. How about your grandad?
RUSSELL. I never had one.
JULIE. Funny that when you knew my husband you thought he was obsessed with gardening. I always thought he was obsessed with girls' bums.
SUKI. Really?

PRUE. Oh, yes, he was always a keen wobbler.
MATT. What do you mean? How do you know?
PRUE. Oh, don't get excited. It's all in the past.
MATT. What is?
SUKI. I sometimes feel that the past is never past.
RUSSELL. What do you mean?
JULIE. You mean that yesterday is today?
SUKI. That's right. You feel the same, do you?
JULIE. I do.
MATT. Bollocks.
JULIE. I wouldn't like to live again though would you? Once is more than enough.
LAMBERT. I'd like to live again. In fact I'm going to make it my job to live again. I'm going to come back as a better person, a more civilized person, a gentler person, a nicer person.
JULIE. Impossible.

(Pause.)

PRUE. I wonder where these two met. I mean Lambert and Suki.
RUSSELL. Behind a filing cabinet.

(Silence.)

JULIE. What is a filing cabinet?
RUSSELL. It's a thing you get behind.

(Pause.)

LAMBERT. No, not me, mate, You've got the wrong bloke. I agree with my wife. I don't even know what a filing cabinet looks like. I wouldn't know a filing cabinet if I met one coming around the corner.

(Pause.)

JULIE. So what's your job now then, Suki?

SUKI. Oh, I'm a schoolteacher now. I teach infants.

PRUE. What, little boys and little girls?

SUKI. What about you?

PRUE. Oh, Julie and me — we run charities. We do charities.

RUSSELL. Must be pretty demanding work.

JULIE. Yes, we're at it day and night, aren't we?

PRUE. Well, there are so many worthy causes.

MATT. *(To RUSSELL.)* You're a banker? Right?

RUSSELL. That's right

MATT. *(To LAMBERT.)* He's a banker.

LAMBERT. With a big future before him.

MATT. Well, that's what he reckons.

LAMBERT. I want to ask you a question. How did you know he was a banker?

MATT. Well, it's the way he holds himself, isn't it?

LAMBERT. Oh yes.

SUKI. What about you two?

LAMBERT. Us two?

SUKI. Yes.

LAMBERT. Well, we're consultants, Matt and me. Strategy consultants.

MATT. Strategy consultants.

LAMBERT. It means we don't carry guns. *(MATT and LAMBERT laugh.)* We don't have to!

MATT. We're peaceful strategy consultants.

LAMBERT. Worldwide. Keeping the peace.

RUSSELL. Wonderful.

LAMBERT. Eh?

RUSSELL. Really impressive. We need a few more of you about. *(Pause.)* We need more people like you. Taking responsibility. Taking charge. Keeping the peace. Enforcing the peace. Enforcing peace. We need more like you. I think I'll have a word with my bank. I'm moving any minute to a more substantial bank. I'll have a word with them. I'll suggest lunch. In the City. I know an ideal restaurant. All the waitresses have big tits.

SUKI. Aren't you pushing the tits bit a bit far?

RUSSELL. Me? I thought you did that.

(Pause.)

LAMBERT. Be careful. You're talking to your wife.
MATT. Have some respect, mate.
LAMBERT. Have respect. That's all we ask.
MATT. It's not much to ask.
LAMBERT. But it's crucial.

(Pause.)

RUSSELL. So how is the strategic consultancy business these days?
LAMBERT. Very good, old boy. Very good.
MATT. Very good. We're at the receiving end of some of the best tea in China.

(RICHARD and SONIA come to the table with a magnum of champagne, the WAITER with a tray of glasses. Everyone gasps.)

RICHARD. To celebrate a treasured wedding anniversary.

(MATT looks at the label on the bottle.)

MATT. That's the best of the best.

(The bottle opens. RICHARD pours.)

LAMBERT. And may the best man win!
JULIE. The woman always wins.
PRUE. Always.
SUKI. That's really good news.
PRUE. The woman always wins.

(RICHARD and SONIA raise their glasses.)

RICHARD. To the happy couple. God bless. God bless you all.
EVERYONE. Cheers. Cheers ...
MATT. What a wonderful restaurant this is.

SONIA. Well, we do care. I will say that. We care. That's the point. Don't we?

RICHARD. Yes. We do care. We care about the welfare of our clientele. I will say that.

(LAMBERT stands and goes to them.)

LAMBERT. What you say means so much to me. Let me give you a cuddle. *(He cuddles RICHARD.)* And let me give you a cuddle. *(He cuddles SONIA)* This is so totally rare, you see. None of this normally happens. People normally — you know — people normally are so distant from each other. That's what I've found. Take a given bloke — this given bloke — this given bloke doesn't know that another given bloke exists. It goes down through history, doesn't it?

MATT. It does.

LAMBERT. One bloke doesn't know that another bloke exists. Generally speaking. I've often noticed.

SONIA. *(To JULIE and PRUE.)* I'm so touched that you're sisters. I had a sister. But she married a foreigner and I haven't seen her since.

PRUE. Some foreigners are all right.

SONIA. Oh, I think foreigners are charming. Most people in this restaurant tonight are foreigners. My sister's husband had a lot of charm but he also had an enormous mustache. I had to kiss him at the wedding. I can't describe how awful it was. I've got such soft skin, you see.

WAITER. Do you mind if I interject?

RICHARD. I'm sorry?

WAITER. Do you mind if I make an interjection?

RICHARD. What on earth do you mean?

WAITER. Well, it's just that I heard all these people talking about the Austro-Hungarian Empire a little while ago and I wondered if they'd ever heard about my grandfather. He was an incredibly close friend of the Archduke himself and he once had a cup of tea with Benito Mussolini. They all played poker together, Winston Churchill included. The funny thing about my grandfather was that the palms of his hands always seemed to be burning. But his eyes were

elsewhere. He had a really strange life. He was in love, he told me once, with the woman who turned out to be my grandmother, but he lost her somewhere. She disappeared, I think, in a sandstorm. In the desert. My grandfather was everything men aspired to be in those days. He was tall, dark and handsome. He was full of goodwill. He'd even give a cripple with no legs crawling on his belly through the slush and mud of a country lane a helping hand. He'd lift him up, he'd show him his way, he'd point him in the right direction. He was like Jesus Christ in that respect. And he was gregarious. He loved the society of his fellows, W. B. Yeats. T. S. Eliot, Igor Stravinsky, Picasso, Ezra Pound, Bertolt Brecht, Don Bradman, the Beverly Sisters, the Inkspots, Franz Kafka, and the Three Stooges. He knew these people where they were isolated, where they were alone, where they fought against savage and pitiless odds, where they suffered vast wounds to their bodies, their bellies, their legs, their trunks, their eyes, their throats, their breasts, their balls —
    LAMBERT. *(Standing.)* Well, Richard — what a great dinner!
    RICHARD. I'm so glad.

(LAMBERT opens his wallet and unpeels fifty-pound notes. He gives two to RICHARD.)

    LAMBERT. This is for you.
    RICHARD. No, no really —
    LAMBERT. No, no, this is for you. *(To SONIA.)* And this is for you.
    SONIA. Oh, no, please —

(LAMBERT dangles the notes in front of her cleavage.)

    LAMBERT. Shall I put them down here? *(SONIA giggles.)* No, I'll tell you what — you wearing suspenders? *(SONIA giggles.)* Stick them in your suspenders. *(To WAITER.)* Here you are, son. Mind how you go. *(Puts a note into his pocket.)* Great dinner. Great restaurant. Best in the country.
    MATT. Best in the world, I'd say.
    LAMBERT. Exactly. *(To RICHARD.)* I'm taking their bill.

RUSSELL. No, no, you can't —
LAMBERT. It's my wedding anniversary! Right? *(To RICH-ARD.)* Send me their bill.
JULIE. And his.
LAMBERT. Send me both bills. Anyway.... *(He embraces SUKI.)* It's for old time's sake as well, right?
SUKI. Right.
RICHARD. See you again soon?
MATT. Absolutely.
SONIA. See you again soon.
PRUE. Absolutely.
SONIA. Next celebration?
JULIE. Absolutely.
LAMBERT. Plenty of celebrations to come. Rest assured.
MATT. Plenty to celebrate.
LAMBERT. Dead right.

(MATT slaps his thighs.)

MATT. Like — who's in front? Who's in front?

(LAMBERT joins in the song, slapping his thighs in time with MATT.)

LAMBERT and MATT.
Who's in front?
Who's in front?
LAMBERT.
Get out of the bloody way
You silly old cunt.

(LAMBERT and MATT laugh.
SUKI and RUSSELL go to their table to collect handbag and jacket,
    etc.)

SUKI. Sweet of him to take the bill, wasn't it?
RUSSELL. He must have been very fond of you.
SUKI. Oh, he wasn't all that fond of me really. He just liked my

... oh, you know ....
RUSSELL. Your what?
SUKI. Oh, my ... you know ....
LAMBERT. Fabulous evening.
JULIE. Fabulous.
RICHARD. See you soon then.
SONIA. See you soon.
MATT. I'll be here for breakfast tomorrow morning.
SONIA. Excellent!
PRUE. See you soon.
SONIA. See you soon.
JULIE. Lovely to see you.
SONIA. See you soon, I hope.
RUSSELL. See you soon.
SUKI. See you soon.

(They drift off.)

JULIE'S VOICE. So lovely to meet you.
SUKI'S VOICE. Lovely to meet you.

(Silence.
The WAITER stands alone.)

WAITER. When I was a boy my grandfather used to take me to the edge of the cliffs and we'd look out to sea. He bought me a telescope. I don't think they have telescopes anymore. I used to look through this telescope and sometimes I'd see a boat. The boat would grow bigger through the telescopic lens. Sometimes I'd see people on the boat. A man, sometimes, and a woman, or sometimes two men. The sea glistened.

My grandfather introduced me to the mystery of life and I'm still in the middle of it. I can't find the door to get out. My grandfather got out of it. He got right out of it. He left it behind him and he didn't look back.

He got that absolutely right.

And I'd like to make one further interjection.

(He stands still.)

(Slow fade.)

ABOUT THE AUTHOR

Harold Pinter was born in London in 1930. He is married to Antonia Fraser. In 1995 he was awarded the David Cohen British Literature Prize for a lifetime's achievement in literature. In 1996 he was given the Laurence Olivier Award for a lifetime's achievement in theater.